I See and See

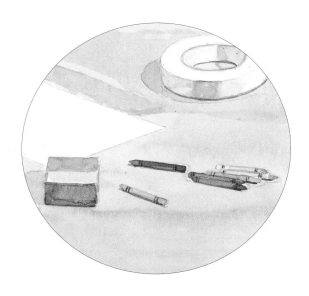

I See and See

TED LEWIN

I Like to Read®

HOLIDAY HOUSE • NEW YORK

I Like to Read® books, created by award-winning picture book artists as well as talented newcomers, instill confidence and the joy of reading in new readers.

We want to hear every new reader say, "I like to read!"

Visit our website for flash cards, activities, and more about the series:
www.holidayhouse.com/ILiketoRead
#ILTR
This book has been tested by an educational expert and determined to be a guided reading level B.

To all my good friends at Holiday House

The child's drawings were created by Ernado J. Villanueva Jr., who was also the model for this book.

I LIKE TO READ is a registered trademark of Holiday House Publishing, Inc.

Library of Congress Cataloging-in-Publication Data

Lewin, Ted, author, illustrator.
I see and see / Ted Lewin. — First edition.
pages cm. — (I like to read)
Summary: A boy goes for a walk where he sees a dog,
trucks, flowers, a bird, and other things; and then
goes home to draw them.
ISBN 978-0-8234-3544-9 (hardcover)
[1. Drawing—Fiction.] I. Title.
PZ7.L58419Iam 2016
[E]—dc21
2015015543

ISBN 978-0-8234-3545-6 (paperback)

I see.

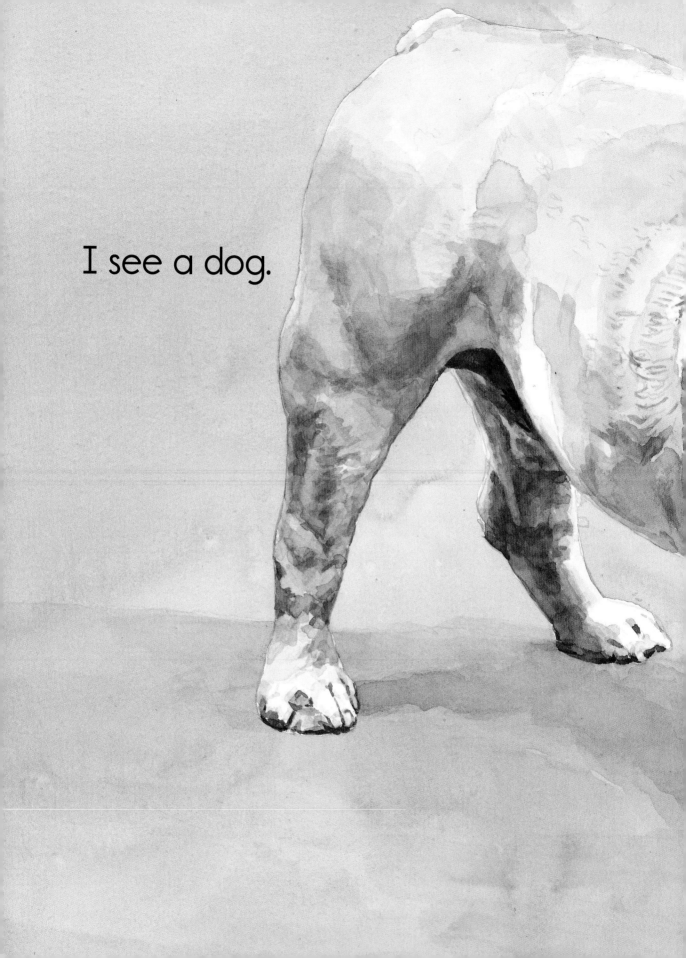

I see a dog.

I see a truck.

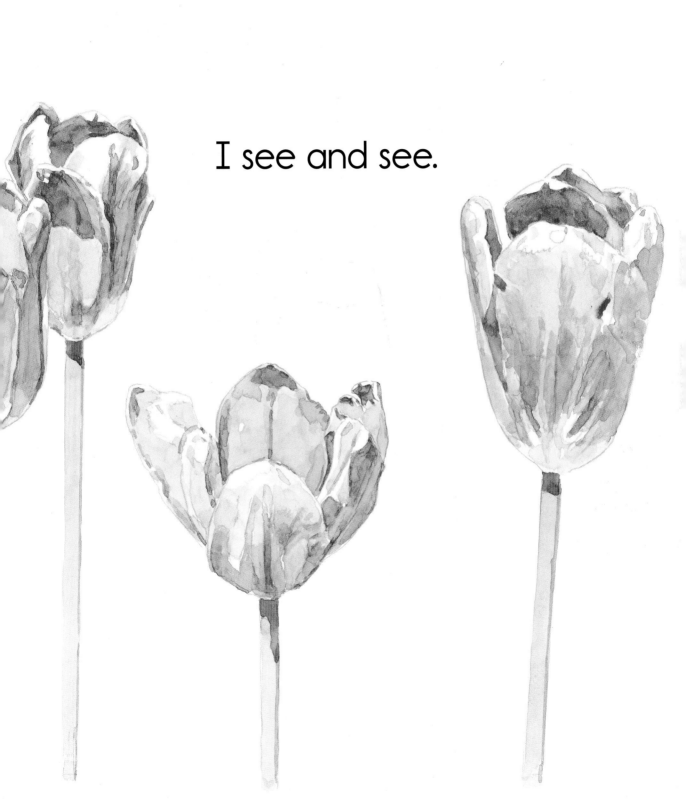

I see and see.

I see a bird.

I see a truck.

I see and see.

I see a man.

I see a truck.

I see and see.

I see and see.

You will like these too!

Come Back, Ben by Ann Hassett and John Hassett
A *Kirkus Reviews* Best Book

Dinosaurs Don't, Dinosaurs Do by Steve Björkman
A Notable Social Studies Trade Book for Young People

Fish Had a Wish by Michael Garland
A *Kirkus Reviews* Best Book
A Top 25 Children's Books list book

The Fly Flew In by David Catrow
Maryland Blue Crab Young Reader Award winner

Little Ducks Go by Emily Arnold McCully
A Bank Street Best Children's Book of the Year

Look! by Ted Lewin
The Correll Book Award for Excellence
in Early Childhood Informational Text

Me Too! by Valeri Gorbachev
A Bank Street Best Children's Book of the Year

Mice on Ice by Rebecca Emberley and Ed Emberley
An IRA/CBC Children's Choice

Pig Has a Plan by Ethan Long
An IRA/CBC Children's Choice

Ping Wants to Play
A Bank Street Best Children's Book of the Year

See Me Dig by Paul Meisel
A *Kirkus Reviews* Best Book

See Me Run by Paul Meisel
A Theodor Seuss Geisel Award Honor Book
An ALA Notable Children's Book

You Can Do It! by Betsy Lewin
A Bank Street Best Children's Book of the Year,
Outstanding Merit

See more I Like to Read® books.
Go to www.holidayhouse.com/I-Like-to-Read/

Some More I Like to Read® Books in Paperback

Animals Work by Ted Lewin

Bad Dog by David McPhail

Big Cat by Ethan Long

Can You See Me? by Ted Lewin

Cat Got a Lot by Steve Henry

Drew the Screw by Mattia Cerato

The Fly Flew In by David Catrow

Happy Cat by Steve Henry

Here Is Big Bunny by Steve Henry

I Have a Garden by Bob Barner

I See and See by Ted Lewin

Little Ducks Go by Emily Arnold McCully

Me Too! by Valeri Gorbachev

Mice on Ice by Rebecca Emberley and Ed Emberley

Not Me! by Valeri Gorbachev

Pig Has a Plan by Ethan Long

Pig Is Big on Books by Douglas Florian

What Am I? Where Am I? by Ted Lewin

You Can Do It! by Betsy Lewin

Visit http://www.holidayhouse.com/I-Like-to-Read/
for more about I Like to Read® books, including flash cards,
reproducibles and the complete list of titles.